D1442130

JACK THE GIANT-KILLER

Jack's First & Finest Adventure

JACK
THE GIANT-KILLER

Jack's First & Finest Adventure
retold in verse
as well as
other useful information about giants
including
How to Shake Hands with a Giant

by Beatrice Schenk de Regniers
Pictures by Anne Wilsdorf

Atheneum **1987** *New York*

For Francis, of course

Atheneum
Macmillan Publishing Company
866 Third Avenue, New York, NY 10022

Type set by Linoprint Composition, New York City
Printed and bound by Toppan Printing Company, Inc., Japan
Typography by Mary Ahern
First Edition

10 9 8 7 6 5 4 3 2 1

Library of Congress Cataloging in Publication Data

De Regniers, Beatrice Schenk.
Jack the giant killer.

SUMMARY: *Retells in verse Jack's encounter with a*
giant, including such lore as the right way to shake
hands with a giant.
[1. Fairy tales. 2. Folklore—England. 3. Giants—
Folklore. 4. Stories in rhyme] I. Wilsdorf, Anne, ill.
II. Title.
PZ8.3.D443Jae   1987   398.2'1'0941   [E]   86-3606
ISBN 0-689-31218-0

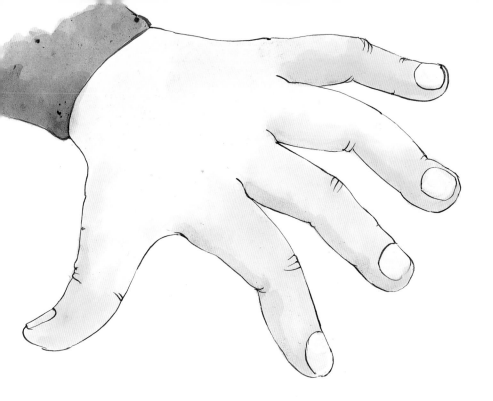

CONTENTS

Jack the Giant-Killer

The people in this story:

A boy named Jack.
He's small but brave.
He lives in Cornwall, England.

A Giant who likes
To rant and rave.
He lives on an island.
(The island is near Cornwall)

Each day when
The sun went down,
The Giant came
To every town
　　and farm in Cornwall.

He came to steal!
　　He stole the corn,
　　He stole the hogs,
　　He stole the sheep,
　　He stole the dogs,
　　　and ate them.

And now and then he even stole
A boy or girl and ate them whole.

Said Jack:
    "This Giant's a monster!
    He must die.
    Now who will dare
    To kill him? I
               will."

Jack takes his shovel
And his horn of tin.
The water is cold,
But Jack jumps in
and swims to the Giant's island.

The night is dark,
The Giant asleep.
Jack digs a pit
Both wide and deep,
Then covers it over
With a heap
      of sticks and straw.

Jack blows his horn
A good loud blast.
The Giant jumps up,
Comes running fast.

"You woke me up.
It's all your fault.
I'll eat you for breakfast
With pepper and salt,"

           he roars.

Is Jack afraid?
No. Not a bit.
He simply stands there,
Near the pit.
The Giant will
Fall into it

           if he takes one more step!

"So come and get me,"
Sly Jack calls.
The Giant comes.
The Giant falls
into the pit.

Jack raps the Giant
On the head.
The wicked Giant
Is very dead.

Now Jack swims home.
"He's back! He's back!"
The people shout.
"Hurrah for Jack
    the Giant-Killer."

People who believed in Giants
used to say...

A cave is
the hollow bone
of a giant's leg.

Thunder is the
sound of a giant
laughing.

Lakes are a giant's
footprints filled with
water.

Sand dunes and great boulders
show where a giant emptied
the sand and gravel out
of his shoes.

Mist or fog rising from a mountain
is the smoke from a giant's pipe.

A strong wind means
a giant is blowing on
his soup to cool it.

Earthquakes happen
when a giant sneezes so hard
he shakes the earth.

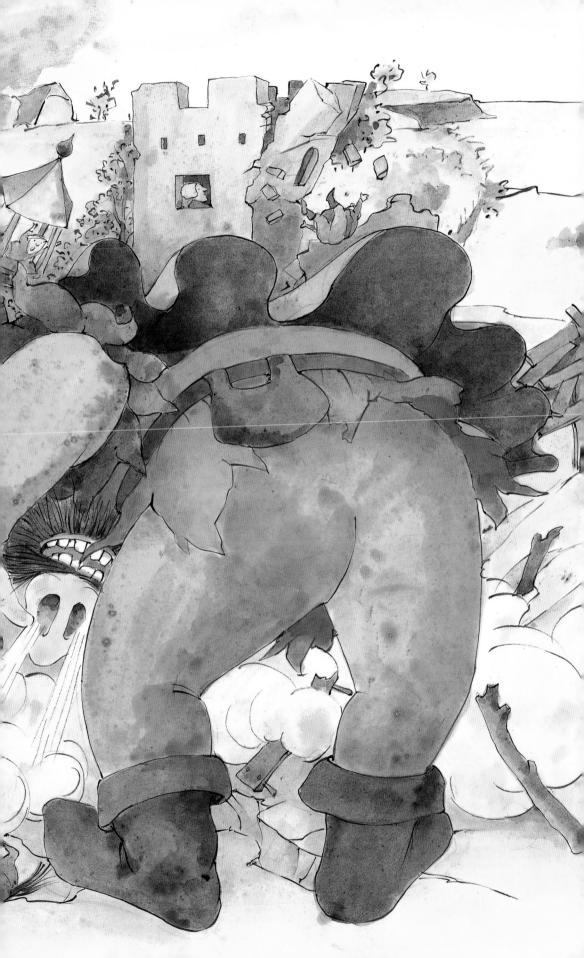

How to Shake Hands with a Giant
(if you ever want to use your hand again)

Always carry an iron rod with you
if you are in giant country.
Then if you meet a giant
who wants to shake hands with you,
just hold out the iron rod.

If there is a fire handy,
stick the rod in the fire first
until it gets red hot.
The giant will like that.